# DARK
## - BOOK 2-

# WOLF
# SQUAD

# CAMERON ALEXANDER

BICKERING
OWLS
PUBLISHING

*To my wife, for all of her support.*

Dark Corps series. Wolf Squad
by Cameron Alexander
Published by Bickering Owls Publishing

Cover Art and Book Design by Rhett Pennell

ISBN: 978-0-9991138-3-7

First Printing August 2017

# CONTENTS

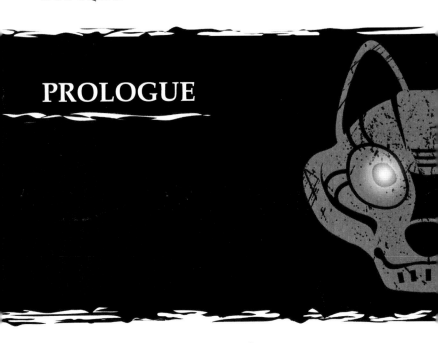

# PROLOGUE

If you've ever read a book with a prologue before, then you should know that it's just a fancy way of saying "a part at the beginning before the story actually starts." Usually a prologue introduces you to something, and then you have to remember that something because it's going to be important later.

Sometimes a prologue can also mean "an

event that leads to another event." This prologue, the one you're reading right now, is both: it's a part at the beginning before the story actually starts, but it's also an event that will lead to another event later.

If any of that sounded confusing to you, that's good. You're not supposed to know what's going on right now. The only thing you're supposed to do is pay attention, remember what happens here, and keep reading.

The city was under siege—which is just another way of saying that it was being attacked. And even though the city was being attacked, most people didn't know it at all. They went about their normal business, going to work and shopping for groceries and seeing movies, without any idea at all that their fair city was under siege.

The reason that no one knew the city was

being attacked was because the attackers were barely more than shadows—slithering, sneaking, creeping, crawling shadowy figures called the Dark. They swept into the city under the safety of night and they scattered, searching for someone. They were looking for a boy.

The problem was that the Dark was not from this world, the world that you live in, so they weren't sure exactly what this boy looked like. Sometimes they thought that adults were boys, or that girls were boys, or even that dogs and fire hydrants might be the boy. Still they searched, using the one advantage they had: the Dark could smell fear. They could smell it the same way that you or I might smell bacon sizzling in a pan, and they followed the scent, because they believed that the boy they were looking for was alone and afraid.

And if you think all that is strange, we're

just getting started. Late at night, in a storage facility on the far side of the city, four wolves were opening a storage unit with a tall, rolling orange door.

"What was the combination again?" asked one of the four wolves. Yes, you read that right; these wolves could speak. They also stood upright on two legs, and they wore gray armor that covered their entire body, head to toe. The wolf that spoke had blue glowing eyes that were currently staring up at a combination lock, because each of these wolves stood only two feet tall.

"One-nine-four-six," said another wolf. This one had green, glowing eyes and he looked around, watching the area to make sure no one saw them.

"Flashers," muttered a wolf with red eyes. "Why flashers?"

"That's what the general said," the green-eyed wolf told him. "He said to get flashers, so that's what we're doing." He sniffed the air, catching a whiff of something odd. Wolves have an excellent sense of smell, and these wolves were no exception. "Hey, do you smell that? It smells like… like… there was a battle here."

The fourth wolf, this one with purple glowing eyes, sniffed the air and said, "Smells like cheese to me."

"No, not cheese." The green-eyed wolf sniffed again. "I think Bear Company was here. And I think they were in a fight. The Dark must have attacked them."

"I hope they're okay," said the red-eyed wolf.

"I hope Timmy is still with them," said the blue-eyed wolf.

"I hope there's really cheese around here,"

said the purple-eyed wolf.

They opened the storage unit, which looked like it was filled with ordinary junk, except that it had a very secret compartment far in the back. And in that secret compartment were weapons—but not the sort of weapons you might think. These weapons were called flashers, and they shot beams of light from them.

"There are six flashers missing," said the blue-eyed wolf. "Bear Company *was* here."

The wolves each took a flasher and attached them to their wrists. The green-eyed wolf, who was the leader, took one extra flasher just in case. Then they closed the secret compartment and the storage unit. "Come on," said the green-eyed wolf. "We need to find the bears and help them however we can—"

Before he could finish his sentence, the wolves saw a blur of movement to their left. All four of them spun suddenly, just in time to see a shadow fly by, so quick it was hard to see it.

"The Dark!" shouted the red-eyed wolf.

"Shoot it!" the purple-eyed wolf said excitedly.

"No." The green-eyed wolf shook his head. "It must have gotten separated from the others during their battle. Don't shoot it; let's follow it and see where it goes."

"But it might lead us to wherever the rest of the Dark are!" said the blue-eyed wolf.

"Maybe. But it might lead us to Bear Company and Timmy. Wolf Squad, move out!" The green-eyed wolf and his three companions hurried after the fleeing shadow.

# CHAPTER 1:

# THE STORY SO FAR

Every story has a beginning, and every beginning usually starts with the first chapter. This book, however, is a little bit different, because this is the first chapter, but the story does not start here. Actually, this story started with the first chapter of a whole other book, and if you haven't yet read that story, then you should definitely go back and read that one first—because that's where the story starts.

If you've already read that first book, then you already know that this story is about a young boy, a famous scientist, five stuffed bears… and the things that lurk in the shadows.

You see, about a month ago, a renowned scientist named Dr. Barnes was kidnapped and put in a big white room with no windows in a secret underground research lab. As if that wasn't bad enough, he was then forced to build a portal, or a doorway, to another dimension, which is a world that we can't see but exists at the same time as our world. It's all very scientific stuff, and while we could probably spend an entire book just talking about that and using complicated terms like "interdimensional" and "space-time continuum," we really want to stick to this story, so for now let's just say that the portal worked, and a doorway was opened between our world and another one.

And what came through it was not good at all.

Dr. Barnes's portal let in a slew of inky-black creatures called the Dark, shape-shifting shadows that can bond with everyday stuff and make it a part of them. For example, the Dark could bond with a spatula, and then they would have a spatula for an arm—although that wouldn't be very useful unless they were flipping hamburgers, or maybe for swatting flies.

The Dark was led by a big, bad shadow called Total Dark, who took one look at our bright, vibrant world and decided that he wanted to take it over. The problem is that only a few hundred of his minions came through the portal before Dr. Barnes shut it down, and while the Dark are very fast and quite frightening, that's still not nearly enough to take over all of Earth.

So Total Dark came up with a plan: he would force Dr. Barnes to build a new doorway, a much bigger one, and let millions of his minions come through so that he can take over Earth and make our bright little planet into a dark, miserable place like his world.

Of course, Dr. Barnes said no. He wasn't afraid of the Dark, and besides, helping them to take over our planet would definitely ruin his plans for the summer. But Total Dark could smell fear, so he knew that there was one thing that the doctor was afraid of. The only thing that Dr. Barnes feared in the whole world was that something terrible might happen to his young son, Timmy.

Total Dark was generally a not-so-nice guy, so he sent a dozen of his minions after Timmy. But Dr. Barnes was as smart as he was fearless, and he had a contingency—which is a fancy way of saying "back-up plan." You see, Dr. Barnes had left his ten-year-old son with five stuffed bears. They seemed like ordinary toys; nothing special about them, except that each of them had a hard metal case on their back.

When the Dark came out of the portal, Dr. Barnes activated the five bears, who came to life (much to Timmy's surprise, of course). The hard cases on their backs opened up and wrapped the plush bears in magnificent, shining armor. The five bears together were called Bear Company, and they had only one goal: to keep Timmy safe from any threat while they brought him to his father.

The leader of Bear Company was the red bear, whose name was Mother. She was kind, brave, and fearless. All of the other bears looked up to her to show them the way.

Then there was the green bear, Bruiser. He

liked to fight, and even though the bears were only two feet tall, Bruiser was fierce—though his answer to every problem was usually to charge in and beat everyone up.

Sneak was the orange bear, and he got his name by being able to move around without a sound. He was the scout of Bear Company. But there was something wrong with his hardware, and every once in a while he would make a high-pitched noise that sounded like a half-hiccup, half-sneeze. *"Heek!"*

The blue bear was called Keylogger, but Timmy just called him Blue. He was a computer expert and could hack into just about anything that was digital.

Lastly there was Patch, the yellow bear, who was the medic of Bear Company. She could fix up anyone, human or bear. She also told really bad jokes when she was nervous.

Together, Bear Company and Timmy made their way halfway across the city to get their weapons, light cannons they called flashers, which shot pure light in balls and beams—a most excellent weapon against the Dark. But the bears were attacked while they were trying to cross a junkyard, and one of Total Dark's minions, whose name was Shroud, bonded with all sorts of sharp metal to protect himself from the flashers.

Mother managed to defeat Shroud by supercharging her flasher beam to a dangerous level. Her flasher exploded, and Timmy thought he had lost her. Luckily, she was okay, but her armor was very badly damaged, so Timmy and Bear Company were forced to hide in the junkyard during the day while Patch fixed Mother.

And now you know the story so far—or most of it. If you haven't read the first book, you really should go back and take a look, because there's a lot more to it than just that. There are bad jokes and sneezing bears, scientists and secret agents, sewers and shadows and security guards. This part is just what we call a recap, which is a fancy way of saying "here's all the main stuff that happened so far in this story."

If you did already read the first book… what are you waiting for? Turn the page and see what happens next.

# CHAPTER 2:

# SAFE IN THE DAYLIGHT

"**T**immy breathed a sigh of relief as the sun rose over the junkyard. There was not a cloud in the sky; it looked like it would be a very nice spring day. He would have loved to be playing in the park, or napping on a sofa with the windows open, or pretty much anywhere else than in a smelly junkyard filled with huge heaping piles of garbage.

The junkyard wasn't all bad, though. For one, there were plenty of things to hide behind. There were old refrigerators and broken microwaves and ancient, rusting cars. Timmy was pretty certain that no one could find them here. Also, since it was daytime, he was mostly sure that the Dark could not get to them—or at least he hoped.

"We shouldn't stay here," said Bruiser, shaking his head. "We should keep moving. We could be out of the city before night falls."

"Absolutely not," said Patch. The yellow bear was tinkering with the metal case on Mother's back. "Not while Mother is defenseless." Mother had supercharged her flasher beam to defeat the shadow called Shroud, and when her flasher exploded, she had pulled back her armor so that her plushy stuffed-bear body absorbed most of the impact. Unfortunately, her armor was not working, and Mother's fur was singed black in many places.

"Patch is right," Mother agreed. "I'm no good to us like this."

"Besides," said Blue, "where would we go? We can't go into the sewers again—there's no sunlight down there. The Dark might find us. And if we stay up here, people might see us. It's too risky."

"I don't think anyone will find us here," Timmy said. "There's lots of stuff to hide behind."

"I hate waiting," Bruiser grumbled. "And I hate hiding."

Timmy stomach growled loudly. He hadn't eaten anything since dinner the day before, and now it was just around breakfast time. Sneak, the orange bear, heard the rumble.

"Oh, right," said Sneak. "I guess you need to

eat, don't you?" The bears didn't need to eat or sleep or drink water or use the bathroom or any of those things like people do. Even though they could talk and walk and learn, and they each had their own personality, they weren't really alive; they were something else. Timmy didn't want to call them "robots" because that didn't seem right. His father had built them to look like ordinary stuffed toys, but when he activated them, they came alive and sprouted their shining armor and glowing eyes and mechanical fingers at the end of their paws.

His father had used a term before called "artificial intelligence," which meant that Bear Company could do all the things that people could, but they weren't actually living things. It all seemed very complicated to Timmy, but he knew enough not to call them robots. Instead, he just called them friends.

His stomach rumbled again, louder this time, loud enough for all five bears to hear.

"Hmm," said Mother. "We need to find something for you to eat. I suppose you should also get some sleep while we're here. You were awake all night."

It was true; not only was he hungry, but he was also very tired. Bear Company had activated last night; it was Sneak's half-hiccup, half-sneeze that woke Timmy, and then he and the bears had escaped from the house in the city, traveled through the sewers, and into the junkyard.

"That's not the only problem," said Blue. "All this metal in the junkyard is jamming my signals. I can't radio the general."

Mother frowned. "That's no good. We need to report to him and let him know what happened here."

You see, Bear Company had two goals.

The first goal, and the most important part of the mission, was to keep Timmy safe at all costs. Mother had already proven that when she supercharged her flasher beam and almost sacrificed herself to save Timmy.

Their second goal was to get to the rendezvous point, which was just a fancy way to say "the place you meet someone," and the someone that they were supposed to meet was the general. Timmy didn't know who the general was, but he knew that there were others like Bear Company—a lot more. Over the last four years, ever since Timmy was six years old, his father had given him stuffed animals every time they moved, and they moved around a lot. Each time they moved, some of the stuffed toys got left behind, but there were always new ones. And Timmy couldn't help but think that the other toys were like Bear Company and had also been activated.

But there was more; Timmy's dad was also supposed to be at the rendezvous point, if he had managed to escape from that horrible place underground where he was being kept.

"I have a plan," Mother announced. "We're going to have to split up. Patch, you're going to keep trying to fix my armor. Keylogger, I want you to go find a place where you can get a radio signal. Don't go too far, and don't let any people see you."

"You got it," said Blue.

"Sneak, I want you to try to find something for Timmy to eat," said Mother. "You're the quietest and the sneakiest, so I expect that you won't get caught."

"Sure thing!" said Sneak, happy to help.

"Just try not to sneeze, *Squeak*," said Bruiser. Then he rubbed his hands together eagerly. "And what do you want me to do?"

"Timmy is going to get some sleep in the back of that car over there," said Mother. "And you, Bruiser, are going to stand guard and make sure nothing happens to him."

"Aww," Bruiser groaned. "I hate standing guard. It's so *boring*."

"Well, if anything comes along, you can fight them off," Mother told him.

"What are the chances of that happening?" Bruiser sulked.

Mother shrugged. "I'd say they're pretty good. Maybe fifty-fifty."

The green bear thought about it for a moment. "I guess that's okay."

"Alright Bear Company, you have your orders. Timmy, get some rest," said Mother. "You'll need it so that we can get out of the city tonight."

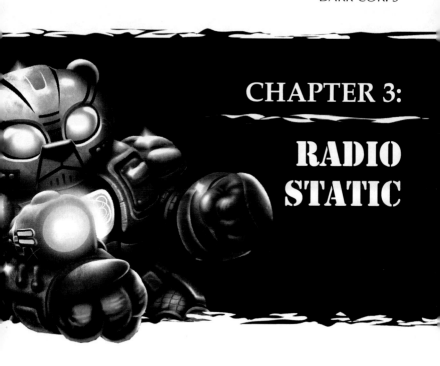

# CHAPTER 3:

# RADIO STATIC

"**H**ey, Mother," said Patch. "What do you do with pineapple ice cream? You put it in a… pinecone!"

"Ha, ha," Mother said sarcastically, which meant that she didn't find the joke funny at all. "Please, Patch. No more bad jokes."

The two of them were hiding behind an old,

rusting dryer. Mother was lying on her soft belly in the gravel while Patch worked on the hard metal case on her back, trying to fix her armor. Patch had already told four bad jokes in the last ten minutes because she was so nervous. And she was nervous because she wasn't sure that a day was long enough to fix Mother.

Dr. Barnes was a very smart man; when he built Patch he made sure that she knew everything there was to know about fixing the members of Bear Company if something happened to them. Because of that, Patch knew that there were six thousand, three hundred and forty-two different pieces inside of Mother, some of them so small you couldn't even see them with a naked eye. Lucky for Patch, her helmet could magnify her vision up to one hundred times, like a microscope, so she could see everything.

But seeing wasn't the problem. The problem

was that Patch would have to check all of those little pieces until she found what was wrong with Mother's armor, and that could take a very long time.

A pair of thin pliers extended from Patch's left bracer, which is just a fancy term for the yellow armor on her wrist. From her right wrist came a skinny black rod with a curved end that was topped with a small blue flame—a welding torch.

Even though Patch very much wanted to tell another joke, instead she concentrated on finding the problem, poking and prodding around in the case while Mother laid flat.

\* \* \*

Blue wandered through the junkyard, being careful to keep an eye out for any people and at the same time checking his radio to see if he got his signal back. But every time he tried the radio, all he got was static that made a sound like: "*Tssssshhhh.*"

"This is no good," he mumbled to himself. "I shouldn't leave the junkyard; someone might see me. But I don't know how to get a signal in here." He looked around for something that might help him.

"Aha!" he said out loud. There was a telephone pole nearby; if he could climb up it, he should be high enough in the air to get a clear signal. Blue stood at the base of the pole and looked up. He wasn't afraid of heights, but it was still a very tall pole. Worse, the rungs of the pole were too far away from each other; he was only a two-foot-tall bear. He would never be able to reach the top.

"Hmm…" he thought. "Maybe I don't have

to climb this pole. If I can get high enough somewhere else…" He looked around. The junkyard was filled with mounds of garbage; he could climb up the highest mound and probably get a signal there.

The highest mound of junk was almost as tall as the telephone pole was. Blue took a deep breath and started to climb. To a small bear, even a fierce armored one, climbing the mound was like climbing a mountain. Every once in a while the junk would shift, and Blue would slide back a few feet, which made it even harder. But he was determined, and it wasn't long before he found himself at the top.

"Huh," he mumbled. "I wish I had a little flag to plant here." He tried to radio the general again by talking into the small black speaker in the palm of his left hand. "General Leo? This is Keylogger from Bear Company. Do you copy?"

"*Tssssshhh…*" All he heard was static.

"General Leo? Do you copy?"

"*Tssssshhh…*"

"This is hopeless!" Blue complained.

Then a voice came through the speaker. "Keylogger? *Tsssh.* I copy."

"General!" Blue almost shouted with joy. "General, listen. We're still in the city, hiding in a junkyard. We were attacked again by the Dark. Mother is hurt, but she's going to be okay. We can't move yet; we'll have to get out of the city tonight."

"Copy," the general said, which is just radio-talk for "I heard you." "I'll radio *tssshh* Wolf Squad *tssshh…* rendezvous at *tssshh.*"

"General? I can't hear you!" said Blue. "General?"

"*Tssssshhh…*" The signal was gone. At least Blue had gotten his message out—and he had definitely heard the words "Wolf Squad," which was very good news. It meant that Bear Company would have reinforcements.

Blue turned off the radio and started his climb down the junk mound to tell Mother.

# CHAPTER 4:

# JUNKYARD DOGS

$S$neak was silent and stealthy as he dashed around the junkyard. First he hid behind a long piece of plywood and peeked around the corner. There was no one in sight. He ran quickly to an overturned lawn mower, tucked into a roll, and hid there for a moment. He checked again; still no one there.

To him, being a scout was about much

more than sneaking around. It was an art form; if you wanted to be a good scout, you had to be graceful and quiet and keep your eyes open at all times. Bruiser would never understand, which is probably why he and Sneak argued so much. Bruiser would rather march right out into the open and shout, "I'm here!" and then try to fight everybody off. To Sneak, that was just plain dumb.

At the far end of the junkyard he found a small building, not much bigger than a shed. "That's probably an office for this place," he said quietly to himself. "There must be some food in there." After checking to make sure the coast was clear, he sprinted to the small building and tried the doorknob. It wasn't locked (which was too bad, because the only thing that Sneak enjoyed more than sneaking was picking locks).

He very carefully crept inside. The office

was quite small; there was a metal desk and a chair, and another door on the other side, and—aha!—there was a very small refrigerator in the corner that was about as tall as Sneak.

He crept toward the refrigerator and was very nearly there when he heard the sound of water running. Then a lock turned. Someone else was there!

Sneak had no time to run or hide. Instead he pulled back his armor, which made a sound like *shooop*, and stayed completely still so that he looked like just an ordinary stuffed bear.

He was just in time, too; exactly one second later a man with a long beard opened the second door in the small building, which led to a bathroom. The man came out and went over to the desk, but then he stopped suddenly, because he very nearly stepped on Sneak.

"How did you get in here?" he asked as he

reached down to pick up the bear. Of course Sneak didn't answer; he was pretending to be a toy. "Is someone else here?" The man looked around but didn't see anyone. "Oh well." He set Sneak down on his desk and then opened the office door to go outside.

Sneak felt a tickle in his nose. He just couldn't help it.

*"Heek!"*

He sneezed.

The man stopped and spun around. Sneak stayed perfectly still, hoping desperately that he wouldn't sneeze again. The man stood there for a long time, staring at Sneak. Then he finally turned and headed outside, closing the office door behind him.

"Phew!" said Sneak. "That was too close." He put his armor back on—which made a sound like *zip-zip!*—and jumped off the desk to the small refrigerator. Inside was a brown paper bag, and inside the bag there was a sandwich, an apple, and a can of soda.

"Bingo!" said Sneak. He took the bag and left the office, making sure that the man wasn't around first. He did feel a little bit bad about stealing the man's lunch, but keeping Timmy safe was part of his mission, and making sure Timmy didn't go hungry was part of keeping Timmy safe.

* * *

Bruiser was bored.

Timmy was safe, fast asleep in the back of the old broken-down station wagon behind him. But Bruiser hated standing guard. He hated waiting around. He wished that something would come along that he could fight.

First he paced for a little while, kicking at the gravel with his small bear feet. Then he got bored of that, so he practiced punching the air, pretending that he was surrounded by foes.

"Hyah! Yah!" He karate-chopped at nothing, his hand going *swish* through the air. That gave him an idea; he could find something around here to break. That would make him feel better. He searched around; metal was too tough. He needed a piece of wood, or something that was already half-broken.

He wandered around one of the large mounds nearby. He sifted through some of the junk, trying to find something breakable, when he heard a sound—a low growl.

At first he thought it might have been the Dark, but when Bruiser looked up he saw two huge black dogs, each one taller than he was, and both of them were growling at him.

"Finally!" he said, smiling behind his helmet. "Something to fight!"

The dogs ducked their heads down low and flattened their ears against their head.

"You want a piece of me?" said Bruiser. "How about a little taste of THIS!" He fired his flasher at the dog on the left. A burst of blue light blasted from the end of it and struck the dog… but did nothing at all, except make the dog growl louder.

"Oh, right," said Bruiser. "Light doesn't hurt dogs. It looks like we'll have to do this the old-fashioned way." He balled his small fists, ready for a fight.

\* \* \*

Timmy had been sleeping soundly in the back of the old station wagon, using his backpack as a pillow. He was woken by a lot of noise outside of the car, and sat up to look out the window.

He rubbed his eyes at the scene in front of him, just to make sure that he was actually awake and not dreaming.

One huge black dog had Bruiser pinned under his paws and was gnawing on the bear's helmet. A second black dog had his teeth clamped around Bruiser's left leg and was trying to pull on it. Both dogs' tails were swishing in the air happily.

Bruiser was shouting and struggling to move, but he was trapped under the weight of the big dog. "Get off of me! Get him off! Someone help!" Of course the dogs' teeth weren't strong enough to pierce his armor, but they were also slobbering all over him.

Sneak and Blue were both nearby, but neither of them were helping; they were laughing so hard they were rolling on their backs in the gravel.

"They think you're a toy!" Sneak said, giggling. "They just want to play with you, Bruiser!"

"It's not funny!"

"It's *very* funny!" Blue said, laughing with his small legs kicking in the air.

Timmy climbed out of the back of the car. The two dogs bounded over to him, their tails wagging. They pushed their big heads against him, wanting to be petted.

"Aw, they're good dogs," said Timmy, patting them each on the head.

"Good dogs?!" said Bruiser. "They slobbered all over me! Look at my armor!"

Sneak started giggling all over again. "Well, at least we know that when all this is over, you can always get a job as a chew toy!"

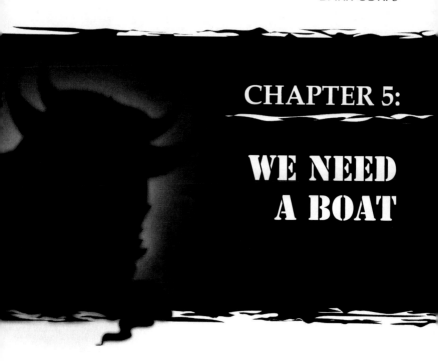

# CHAPTER 5:

# WE NEED
# A BOAT

**V**ery far from the city, near the top of the world, was a place that was all white and blue, for miles and miles in every direction. It was a vast, frozen plain of tundra with almost nothing there—almost, because there was something there, and that something was a very small, very square building made of black brick.

Inside the building there was only one small

room, which was not a room at all but an elevator. That elevator would take you down, down, down—a half-mile down below the surface of Earth, and then its doors would open and you would be in a secret underground research facility.

There were many rooms and chambers in this underground lab, and in each room there was usually some kind of experiment going on. But just last night, Dr. Barnes, Timmy's father, had been forced to open his portal and let the Dark into our world. They swept out through the doorway and quickly took over the underground research base. Now there was only one experiment going on.

In a wide white room filled with complex-looking gadgetry and mechanical whatchamacallits, Dr. Barnes and his research assistant, a young scientist named Arjun, worked to build a second portal. Total Dark had demanded that they build him a larger, more powerful doorway to his world so that more of his minions could come through and help him take over the earth. Dr. Barnes, however, had a secret: even though he was building a new portal, he had no intention of building the one that Total Dark wanted him to build.

"Arjun," said Dr. Barnes to his young partner, "why don't you get some rest? You've been working for hours. There's a cot over there in the corner."

"Thank you, Doctor," said Arjun, "but the faster we can build this portal, the faster we can get out of here."

"I respect your work ethic, Arjun, but you're no good to me if you're exhausted. Please, my friend; take a nap, even if only a brief one."

You see, Dr. Barnes's plan was not to build

a portal that would open to the Dark's world, or any other world, for that matter; his plan was to build a portal that would fold space-time in such a way that it would open here on Earth—but somewhere that was very far away from the underground research lab.

Arjun yawned and nodded, agreeing with the doctor that it would be much better if he could rest, even if just for a short while.

"Doctor," said Arjun, "before I rest, I thought of something that may be a problem for us. I'm sure I don't have to remind you that seventy-one percent of the earth is covered by water."

"That is true," said the doctor. "What of it?"

"Well… doesn't that mean that there is a seventy-one percent chance that our portal will drop us in the middle of the ocean?"

"Oh, my," said Dr. Barnes quietly. He had been so busy thinking about Timmy and hoping that his young son was safe that he had overlooked a very simple fact. "Arjun, that is a brilliant observation and a most grievous oversight on my part. I'm glad I have you around."

"Thank you, Doctor. Unfortunately, this portal will already take several days to build, and the additional calculations to make sure we come out on dry land will make it much longer."

"Unless…" Dr. Barnes looked around, stroking his chin gently, which he did whenever he was deep in thought. "Unless we build a boat."

"A boat?" Arjun repeated.

"A boat," Dr. Barnes confirmed. "My desk over there is mostly made of wood; we could fashion a small boat from it and bring it through the portal with us. If we come out in the ocean, we'll be ready; if we come out on dry land, we'll certainly look crazy for having a boat, but it's better to have it and not need it than need it and not have it."

"But how can we build a boat without the Dark knowing what we're doing?" Arjun asked. "Surely Total Dark will see that a boat is not necessary to build a portal."

"Hmm... you're probably right about that. But I'm not sure that the Dark know what a boat is," said Dr. Barnes. "If we don't call it a boat, maybe they won't know—"

The doctor didn't get to finish his thought, because the room suddenly got a little colder, as if someone had opened a window during the wintertime. But Dr. Barnes knew what it meant; it meant that Total Dark had swept silently into the room.

Sure enough, the tall shadow was right behind him. Total Dark loomed about eight feet high, and his shadowy body was little more than a column with a head and four horns protruding from the top. He had no eyes or mouth or any features at all. When he spoke, it was in a terrible, harsh whisper that sounded like a cross between a growling dog and a car driving on gravel.

*"Tell me of your progress, Doctor,"* hissed Total Dark.

Dr. Barnes stood up straight and tall and said, "You know, here on Earth we have a saying that goes, 'Patience is a virtue.' It means that the ability to wait patiently for something is a valuable quality."

Total Dark growled. *"Work faster, or I will turn your son into one of my minions!"*

Dr. Barnes picked some dirt from under one of his fingernails. "Yes, you mentioned that before. How's that going, by the way?" He knew that Bear Company was active, and that Total Dark had sent a dozen minions after them already.

*"It would seem that your silly bears somehow managed to defeat my commander, Shroud. But no matter; I now realize my error. I sent only one dozen minions. This time, I will send TWO dozen minions!"* Total Dark laughed, which sounded a lot more like nails scraping across a chalkboard than an actual laugh.

"Sure," said Dr. Barnes. He looked at his watch. "Go ahead. Send 'em out." Even though he was a half-mile underground, he knew that at this time the sun would be out, and he was fairly sure that the Dark could not be exposed to direct sunlight (which is why he instructed Bear Company to use their flashers against them).

Total Dark may not have known a lot about our world, but he wasn't dumb, either. *"I think you're trying to trick me, Doctor."*

"Me? Never."

*"We shall see. In the meantime—continue*

*work on my portal!"* The tall shadow slithered down the wall, across the floor, and vanished beneath the closed door.

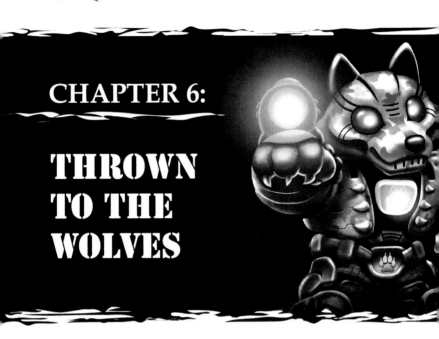

# CHAPTER 6:

# THROWN TO THE WOLVES

**J**onathan was scared. He didn't like being alone in the big house. Actually, he didn't like the big house at all. It made too much noise; the stairs creaked when you walked on them and the pipes banged when the heat came on and sometimes the walls groaned for no reason at all.

He wasn't supposed to be alone in the big house. He was only nine years old, and though there are plenty of nine-year-old children that are very responsible and can probably take care of themselves just fine, and even though Jonathan was one of those responsible nine-year-old children who could take care of himself just fine, it is usually frowned upon to leave nine-year-old children by themselves.

But he wasn't supposed to be alone; Anna was supposed to be here with him. Before she left she told him, "You can come with me. We can leave together."

Jonathan shook his head. "We'll get in trouble."

Anna had sighed. "Well, I'm leaving. You can stay if you want. Don't be scared; I'll send someone to help you, okay? I promise." And then she left.

Jonathan was an orphan, which in case you don't know means that his parents were no longer around. Jonathan's story was a very sad one, so we're not going to go into all that here, because it's bad enough that Jonathan was alone and scared and nine years old in this big house by himself.

The big house was called a foster home, which is a place for children like Jonathan to live for a little while until they get adopted by a nice family. Anna was an orphan too, and she was the only other child in the foster home with Jonathan—for now. The two people that owned this big house, a husband and wife, were called his "foster parents," though they didn't seem very much like parents to him. They weren't very nice to him or to Anna, which was why she left. They didn't let Jonathan play outside unless they were home, and they weren't home very often. In fact, the reason that Jonathan was alone right now was because the man and woman had gone to the orphanage to take in another foster child.

There was plenty of room in the house for more children. It was quite large, right smack in the middle of the city, and it was very old; it was probably here before the tall buildings around it. But even though there were tall buildings on both sides of the old house and those buildings were filled with people, Jonathan still felt very much alone.

His bedroom was on the third floor of the big old house. Alone and with nothing else to do, Jonathan sat on the hardwood floor in his bedroom and played with a small metal car, the only toy he owned in the world. He made car noises and pretended that the floor was a massive superhighway and that each plank of wood was a different lane, and—

The walls groaned, and Jonathan jumped a

little.

He really didn't like the big old house.

He continued to play with his car, but then he heard another noise and he stopped suddenly. It sounded like a door opened and closed somewhere below him. He thought that his foster parents must be home, so he set down his car and went downstairs.

But there was no one there. "Hello?" he called out. His voice sounded very small in the large room. The living room was quite dark; it was always dark in the big old house, because the heavy curtains over the windows were always closed. His foster parents insisted that the curtains always stay closed. They thought there were too many distractions outside in the city. Jonathan often wondered why they didn't live in the countryside instead; they didn't seem to like the city very much at all.

"Hello?" Jonathan called out again.

And then a horrible voice, like a raspy whisper, came to him from somewhere close by. *"Are you afraid of the Dark?"* the terrible voice asked him.

Jonathan gasped and ran out of the living room as fast as he could. He turned the corner and ran into the kitchen, toward the back door, but before he could reach it something stepped into his way and he ran—*SMACK!*—right into the strange something. Jonathan fell over, and so did the something.

"Ow," said Jonathan, rubbing his elbow where he fell.

"You said it," said the something. It sat up. It was a… a… a wolf?

Jonathan shrieked in fear.

"Hey, shh! It's okay." The wolf stood up. Jonathan scrambled away from it, pushing himself across the floor with his hands and feet as he stared at this strange thing. The wolf stood on its back legs and had arms, just like a person, but it was only two feet tall. It was covered in some sort of gray armor with a pattern on it, and its eyes… the wolf's eyes were glowing green.

"I'm not going to hurt you," the wolf said. "My name is Chomper. What's yours?"

"J… J… " Jonathan stammered.

"J.J.?" the wolf asked. "Is your name J.J.?"

"Jonathan," the boy managed to say.

"Jonathan. That's a good name," the wolf said. "Listen, Jonathan. Me and my friends are tracking a dangerous shadow and we saw it come here—probably to hide from the daylight. Have you seen anything strange?"

Jonathan pointed at the wolf and it laughed.

"Besides me," it said.

"There was… something," said Jonathan. "I

didn't see it, but I heard it talk to me."

"Hmm. Okay." The wolf called Chomper turned and shouted, "Wolf Squad! With me!" As Jonathan watched, three other wolves climbed up the stairs from the basement. All four of them looked almost the same, except that their glowing eyes were each a different color. "These are my friends," the green-eyed wolf said. "Wolf Squad, this is Jonathan."

A wolf with purple eyes said, "He looks a little freaked out."

Jonathan nodded. He *was* a little freaked out… but there was also something very friendly about these wolves. He stood up slowly, surprised at how much taller he was than the four wolves. "Who are you?"

"Like I said, we're Wolf Squad," said Chomper. "And it's very important that we find this shadow. I'm sure it's hiding somewhere in this old house. Is anyone else home, Jonathan?"

The boy shook his head, no.

"That's a shame," said the blue-eyed wolf. "Leaving you all alone like that."

"I'm very responsible for my age," Jonathan told them.

"I'm sure you are," said Chomper. "Is it okay with you if we take a look around?"

Jonathan nodded. The four wolves raised their arms; on their wrist was some sort of strange weapon that looked sort of like a flashlight. They carefully checked the living room, where Jonathan had heard the eerie voice, but they found nothing. As they started up the stairs, the wolf leader with the green eyes said, "You can stay down here if you want."

Jonathan nodded. He didn't want to run into the shadow again.

He waited at the bottom of the stairs and

listened. For about a minute or so, there was only silence. Then, suddenly, he heard shouting. Then hissing. Then he saw flashes of light that looked like there was a small lightning storm in the upstairs hall. There was some more hissing, and then a loud screech, and then… silence again.

"What was that?!" Jonathan asked as Chomper and his three wolf friends came back down the stairs.

"That was a shadow that calls itself Blackout," the green-eyed wolf explained. "It escaped, but don't worry; it's weakened, and I don't think it's going to come back."

"Why do you think it came here in the first place?" the red-eyed wolf asked.

Chomper looked at Jonathan. "Fear," the wolf said. "The Dark can smell it. I bet Blackout came here looking for Timmy, and instead found our new friend. I need you to do something for me, Jonathan. Don't be afraid of the Dark, okay?"

"How?" the boy asked. "How can I not be afraid?"

The wolf thought for a moment. Then he said, "Zipper, give me that spare flasher." The red-eyed wolf gave him one of the strange weapons that looked like a flashlight, and Chomper handed it to Jonathan. "This is called a flasher. It shoots beams of light. With this, you'll never have to be afraid of the Dark again."

"Even if I'm alone?" he asked.

"Especially if you're alone. Now we have to go, Jonathan. Our friends are out there, and they need our help. But we're going to come back and check on you again, okay? We promise."

"Wait," said Jonathan. "My friend is out there, too. Her name is Anna, and she's alone. Would you try to find her?"

"We'll try," said Chomper. He turned to the blue-eyed wolf. "The general said that the bears were in a junkyard? What's the fastest way there?"

"We could take the sewers," said the blue-eyed wolf.

"We could hop across the rooftops," offered the red-eyed wolf.

"Or we could steal a car and drive there," said the purple-eyed wolf.

The other three wolves all looked at the purple-eyed one as if he was crazy, but then Chomper shrugged. "You might be right, Nutter. That would be the fastest way." He turned back to Jonathan and said, "It was nice to meet you."

"I hope to see you again," Jonathan said.

"You will. Wolf Squad… let's move out!"

# CHAPTER 7:

# EUREKA!

"**E**ureka!" Patch shouted triumphantly. In case you didn't know, "eureka" is something that smart people shout when they discover something interesting. The first time it was ever used was by a Greek scholar named Archimedes when he discovered that the volume of irregular objects could be precisely measured, which is a fancy way of saying that the water level rises when you get into the bathtub. But that's not terribly important; what's important is that Patch was very smart, and she had discovered something interesting, so she shouted, "Eureka! I've found it!"

"What did you find?" Timmy asked, although it sounded more like "Mmf do ooh fun?" because his mouth was half-full of sandwich at the time.

"I found the part that needs to be fixed," Patch answered. She was still tinkering with the case on Mother's back. "Now it's just a matter of actually fixing it. It shouldn't take me more than an hour or so."

"Nice job, Patch," Mother said, lying on her belly in the gravel. If it was possible for a stuffed bear to get a cramp, Mother would likely have been cramped after several hours of lying down in an uncomfortable position like that. "It looks like we'll be out of this junkyard before nighttime."

"Good thing, too," said Sneak. "There's a man somewhere around here, and I wouldn't want him to find us."

"I have even more good news," said Blue. "I was able to get a little bit of a radio signal by climbing up onto one of the junk heaps. The general is sending Wolf Squad to help us!"

"Who's Wolf Squad?" Timmy asked.

"Eh, just a bunch of rowdy wolves," Bruiser grumbled.

"Don't listen to him," said Sneak. "Wolf Squad is made of some of the best fighters in the whole Dark Corps. Bruiser is just mad because they're better than him."

"Are not!" Bruiser shouted.

"Are too! *Heek!*" Sneak squeaked.

"That's enough, both of you," Mother commanded. "That is good news. Where are we meeting with Wolf Squad?"

"Well… that's the bad news," said Blue. "I couldn't hear what he said, and then I lost the signal. All I heard was 'Wolf Squad.' I guess we'll have to leave the junkyard before we can radio the general again."

"Yes," Mother agreed, "meeting up with Wolf Squad is now our new top priority. Patch will have to finish up first, and then we'll go…" Mother trailed off. "What's that sound?"

Timmy listened intently. The bears had better hearing than he did, but he soon heard it too. It sounded like the engine of a car—and it sounded like it was getting closer.

"Hide!" Mother said. All five of the bears jumped behind the rusted old dryer. Timmy looked left and right for a hiding spot big enough for him to fit. He decided to jump in the backseat of the old station wagon, the one he had been napping in, but before he could close the door behind him a very old red pickup truck drove around the nearest junk heap and rolled to a stop.

The door of the truck opened and the man with the beard got out. "Boy?" he called out. "I saw you, boy. Come on out of there."

Timmy slowly got out of the car. The man frowned at him.

"What are you doing here, kid?" he asked Timmy. "This is no place for a child to be playing. Besides, shouldn't you be in school?"

"I'm home-schooled," Timmy answered.

"Okay, then shouldn't you be at home?" the man asked.

Timmy didn't know what to say. Behind the man, he could see Sneak, Blue and Bruiser peeking out from behind the dryer.

The man with the beard looked around. He didn't see the bears, but he did see the brown paper bag and the mostly-eaten sandwich lying on the ground. "Did you steal my lunch?" the man asked.

"No," Timmy said. It wasn't actually a lie; Sneak was the one that stole the lunch.

"That does it," the man said. "I'm going to have to call someone. It's going to be your parents, or the police. Take your pick."

"You can't call my parents," Timmy said. "My mother passed away and my father is… away for work."

"Then I guess I don't have a choice," said the man. "You stay right there and don't move. I'm going to call the police." He reached into his pocket for a cell phone and began dialing.

At the same time, Sneak very quietly snuck out from behind the dryer. He tiptoed until he was directly behind the bearded man, and then he got down on his hands and knees. Once Sneak was in position, Bruiser jumped out from behind the dryer and shouted, "Boo!"

"Aah!" The man shouted and tried to take a step back, but he tripped over Sneak and fell into the dirt. Blue jumped out from behind the dryer with a length of black rubber tubing. Before the man could get to his feet again, Blue had tied them both of his legs together. Sneak grabbed the cell phone and threw it into a junk heap, while Bruiser tied the man's hands together.

"What is this?" the man cried out. "Who are you? *What* are you?"

"We're really very sorry about all this," said Sneak, "but we didn't want to hurt you, so we're just going to leave you tied up for a little while. Your cell phone is right over there, in that junk pile."

"It'll take you a while, but you can probably crawl over to it," said Blue.

"And by the time you do, we'll be long gone," Bruiser added.

"I must be losing my mind," said the man. He looked at each bear and said, "Hey, was one of you in my office earlier?"

"Yup," said Sneak, " I stole your lunch. Sorry about that, too."

"Bear Company!" Mother called. Her armor still wasn't fixed, but now that the man had spotted them, they had no choice but to move. "Form ranks. Let's get going. Patch will have to finish later."

"Sorry again," Timmy said to the man as they left. "If it helps, that sandwich was very delicious."

"Thank you," said the man. He seemed very calm, considering everything that was happening around him. "My wife made it. As soon as I wake up from this crazy dream, I'll be sure to tell her you said so."

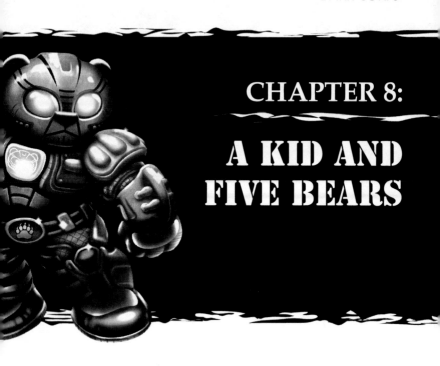

# CHAPTER 8:

# A KID AND FIVE BEARS

**M**s. Gertrude was not very happy.

For starters, she had been assigned to pretend to be a nanny for a young boy named Timothy Barnes. She didn't like children very much, but she did not have a choice, either. The agency wanted someone to look after Timothy, just in case Dr. Barnes refused to build the portal.

It was already bad enough to have to pretend

to be a nanny, but then she woke up this morning to find that Timmy had disappeared in the night. He had run away and left her a short note that said he was going to find his dad.

There was simply no way that a ten-year-old boy could travel all the way to the Arctic, and even if he could, there was no way that he would ever find the small building made of black bricks, and even if he could, there was no way he would take the elevator all the way down to the secret underground research facility, and even if he could, there were so many rooms down there that there was no way he would ever find the one that Dr. Barnes was in.

But even if he could, she knew it would do Timmy no good to travel to the Arctic and find the black building anyway, because the underground base had been compromised, which was a fancy way of saying that someone, or some*thing*, had taken control of it. She did not know what that someone or something was, but she did know one thing: she had to find Timmy. That was her mission.

"He probably didn't even get out of the city yet," Ms. Gertrude said to herself. "He's not old enough to drive a car, and he can't possibly walk very fast on those tiny little child's legs." She had been driving her sleek black car around the city all morning looking for him. She already checked all the places she thought he might be: the park, the playground, the arcade, and the movie theater. He wasn't at any of them.

You see, Ms. Gertrude had been pretending to be Timmy's nanny for the last month, cooking all his meals and making sure he did his schoolwork, but she didn't really know much of anything about children because Ms. Gertrude wasn't really a nanny at all, or a parent, or even an aunt. She was an undercover operative, which is a very fancy way of saying that she was lying to Timmy so that she could keep an eye on him in case his father didn't do what he was supposed to do. Ms. Gertrude always wore a business suit of black slacks, a black blazer, and a crisp white shirt. Her hair was always in a very tight bun on her head. Her nose was sharp and a little crooked, because it had been broken once before and didn't quite heal right.

And she was not very happy, because her job was pretending to be a nanny, not finding missing children.

She turned a dial on her police scanner, which is a device that lets people listen in on radio calls between police officers. She had been listening to it all morning, hoping that someone would report a young boy wandering around the city by himself and carrying five stuffed bears with him.

Ms. Gertrude had no idea why Timmy took the bears with him; all she knew was that when she found that Timmy was missing, she also found an empty shelf where the bears usually were sitting.

Finally, after hours of driving around aimlessly, the police scanner crackled and a voice came through.

"Hey, Joe," said the voice through the radio. "You there?"

"I'm here," said another voice, which was (presumably) Joe.

"Get this," said the first voice. "You know that junkyard on the west side of town? The guy that owns the place just called. He says he found a young kid wandering around by himself."

"Huh," said Joe. "That is strange."

"That's not the strangest part," said the first voice. "He *also* said that the kid had five bears with him."

"Bears?" Joe repeated, probably because he couldn't believe that what he'd heard was right. "You mean like actual bears? The kind in the zoo?"

"No, no," the first voice said. "Little bears, just a couple of feet tall. But he says that the bears were wearing some kind of high-tech armor, and—listen to this—he says that the bears tied him up and ran away with the kid."

"No kidding," said Joe. "You want me to go over and check it out?"

"Yeah," said the voice, "but I'm coming too. I could use a good laugh."

Ms. Gertrude couldn't believe her luck. A young boy with five bears? That was definitely Timmy, no doubt about it. But what was all this about armor and tying people up? What exactly happened in that junkyard?

She was confused, but she was determined to find out. Ms. Gertrude turned her black car around right in the middle of the street and sped off in the opposite direction, toward the junkyard. Timmy couldn't be very far away, and she was going to find him.

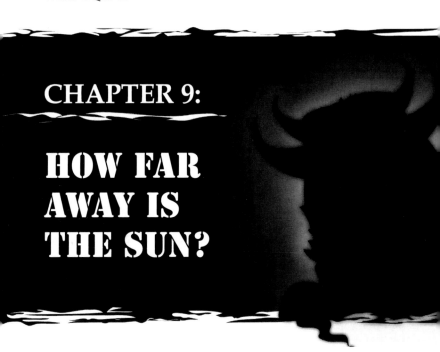

# CHAPTER 9:

# HOW FAR AWAY IS THE SUN?

Total Dark swept into the wide white room so quickly that it felt like a chilly breeze had blown through. Dr. Barnes shivered; it felt colder than normal, which must mean that Total Dark was angry.

*"You DID try to trick me!"* the shadow hissed.

"I don't know what you're talking about,"

said Dr. Barnes, feigning innocence. "Feigning" is just a fancy word that means "faking it," which is exactly what Dr. Barnes was doing—he was faking at being innocent, because he had indeed tried to trick Total Dark into sending his minions outside during the daytime.

*"I sent only one minion out, to see if it was safe,"* Total Dark said, *"and he evaporated! Vanished! What is that bright light? Why is it there? When does it go away?"*

"That, my inky friend, is called the sun," Dr. Barnes explained. "It doesn't go away; at night, the Earth simply rotates so that it isn't shining on this side of the planet anymore."

*"I will destroy this thing you call the sun!"* Total Dark shrieked.

Dr. Barnes chuckled a little.

*"What is so funny?"* the shadow demanded.

"Well, destroying the sun would be very

difficult, and maybe even impossible," the doctor said. "It's very far away and much larger than it looks in the sky."

*"How far away is it?"* Total Dark said. *"The Dark are very fast. I'm sure we will get there in no time!"*

Dr. Barnes chuckled again. "The sun is about ninety-three million miles away. Even if you were going very, very fast, it would still take you many years to reach it. And, of course, that's assuming you can leave Earth's atmosphere. And also assuming you can survive in space. And also assuming you could even get close enough to—"

*"SILENCE!"* Total Dark roared. *"Fine. If I cannot destroy the sun, then I will darken your skies until its light can no longer reach the surface!"*

Dr. Barnes stopped laughing. He wasn't sure if Total Dark really could darken the skies or not, but he didn't want to find out.

*"And because I cannot trust you, Dr. Barnes, I am leaving two of the Dark here as guards."* Two other shadows flew into the room, each of them no larger than an average-sized dog, like a Labrador or a retriever. *"Say hello to my minions, Blot and Pitch."*

"Hello," said Arjun. Dr. Barnes said nothing.

*"They will keep an eye on you while you work,"* Total Dark explained. *"And they will make sure that you're not trying to trick me again."*

Dr. Barnes was worried; there was no way that he and Arjun could build a boat while two of the Dark were watching their every move—unless he could somehow trick them as well, but he would have to come up with a plan for that.

*"Back to work!"* Total Dark ordered. *"And when night comes again, I will send more*

*minions after your son!"* He swept out of the room, leaving the two smaller shadows behind.

"So," Dr. Barnes said once Total Dark was gone. "Blot and Pitch. Which one is which?" One of the small shadows was shorter and round, barely more than a ball-shaped blob with a small head on top. The other was a bit taller, very narrow, and he came to a point at the top, like a pencil.

*"He's Blot..."* said the taller one.

*"And he's Pitch,"* said the shorter fat one.

"I see. Well, I'm Dr. Barnes, and this is my assistant, Arjun."

"Hello," Arjun said again.

*"We know who you are,"* said Blot.

*"And you're supposed to be working,"* said Pitch.

"Right you are," Dr. Barnes agreed. "We'll get back to it."

He picked up a wrench from his workbench. As soon as he did, Pitch swooped up beside him, very close, and hissed, *"What is that? What are you doing?"*

"Um… this is a wrench. I need it to tighten the bolts on the portal's frame," Dr. Barnes explained.

Pitch's shadow flickered a bit, as if he was thinking. *"I suppose that's okay."*

Dr. Barnes thought for a moment, and then he put down the wrench and picked up a pen.

*"What is that thing?"* Blot hissed.

"This is a pen. I need it to do my calculations." Dr. Barnes grabbed a scrap of paper and began writing a note.

*Arjun,* his note said, *I don't believe these creatures are at all familiar with earthly objects. In fact, these two appear to be quite dumb. One of them is watching me right now as I write this, so I don't think they can read English, either. I think we can still build our boat, as long as we do not call it a boat. We will have to pretend that it is an important piece of the portal.*

Dr. Barnes slid the paper across his desk toward his assistant and said, "Arjun, will you please review my calculations to make sure they are accurate?"

Arjun read the note. Then he looked at Blot, and then at Pitch, and then back at Dr. Barnes and said, "Why yes, Doctor, I believe your calculations are very much correct."

"Perfect," said the doctor. "Then let's get back to work."

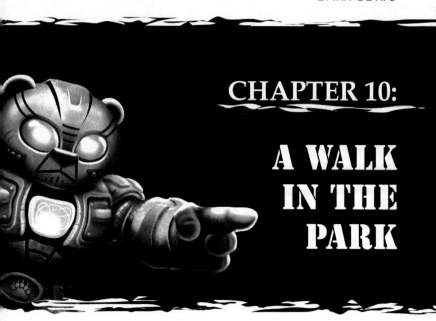

# CHAPTER 10:

# A WALK IN THE PARK

**T**he junkyard was very large, and with all its heaps of garbage it felt very much like a maze, but eventually Timmy and Bear Company found the end of it. The entire junkyard was wrapped in a tall chain-link fence, but Sneak was able to cut a hole in it with a small pair of wire cutters that zipped out from the end of his orange-armored wrist.

"Well," said Bruiser after they had climbed through the fence, "this is no good."

Beyond the fence was a park, a wide stretch of green grass dotted here and there with trees—and unfortunately, plenty of people too.

Blue checked his map of the city, which only he could see through the blue goggles in his helmet. "Across the park is the fastest way to get out of the city."

"How are we ever going to get across it with all these people here?" Patch asked.

"Wait—look! It's a kite-flying day!" said Timmy. It was true; almost everyone in the park had strings in their hands, kites in the air, and they were all looking up.

"So?" asked Sneak.

"So," Timmy explained, "if everyone is busy looking up, then we can run from tree to tree, and if we're lucky, no one will think to look down."

"It's worth a shot," said Mother. She looked very odd with the flasher on her wrist but without her armor, since plushy stuffed bears don't typically carry weapons. "Let's hurry. It's going to be nighttime very soon." She was right; already the sun was hanging low in the sky.

The five bears hid behind the closest tree, a thick sturdy oak, while Timmy acted as a lookout. When everyone was busy looking up at the kites in the sky, he waved his hand and Bear Company hurried to the next tree in a single-file line. Then, when Timmy was once again sure that no one was looking their way, they scrambled to the next tree, and the next.

It was at the fourth tree and about halfway across the park that a little girl around five years old, bored by the kites, looked around and saw a butterfly. She chased it, trying to jump up and grab it—and then she stopped, because straight ahead of her were five small bears running across the field. Her face broke into a wide smile. Then one of the bears, a red one, looked right at her and put its paw to its lips, as if to say, "Shh. Don't tell anyone."

The little girl giggled at the bear, but she didn't say a word.

* * *

"We should be safe now," said Mother. Bear Company and Timmy had made their way across the park to the other side of the city, and were now safely hidden behind a dumpster.

"Safe?" Bruiser blurted out. "Not hardly! Look, it's almost night again!"

He was right; the shadows had grown long while they were crossing the park, and the sky had turned from purple to a dark bluish-black. A few stars were already visible overhead.

"It's okay," said Blue. He was looking at the schematic, or map, of the city in his helmet visor. "We don't have too far to go until we're out of the city."

"And where do we go then?" Timmy asked.

"Don't you worry about that right now," Mother said with a smile. "We need to focus on leaving the city first."

Timmy didn't think that was a very fair answer; he should be allowed to know where they were going and how far they would travel and how long it would take to get there. But he didn't say anything. He trusted Mother.

"Besides, we'll be fine as long as the Dark don't find us," said Sneak.

Bruiser rubbed his hands together. "Oh, I hope they do! I'll fight 'em off, every last one of them."

"Don't say that!" Patch almost shouted. "Mother still isn't fixed; it'll just be four of us against all of them."

"I'll take them all on!" Bruiser said, waving his flasher in the air. "I'm not afraid of anything—"

"Help!"

All five bears, and Timmy, perked up when they heard the cry. It sounded like a young girl, and it sounded close by.

"You all heard that too, right?" Timmy asked, even though he knew the bears could hear much better than he could.

"Help me!" The voice came again, louder.

"It was this way!" Timmy said, and before he knew it, his feet were moving. He was running toward the sound.

"Timmy, wait!" Mother shouted after him.

"It's not safe! Bear Company, follow him!"

Timmy ran without thinking. If he had been thinking, he probably would have thought something like, "Gee, Timmy, you're supposed to be trying to stay *out* of trouble, so it's probably not a very good idea to run *towards* trouble." But, as previously mentioned, he wasn't thinking; all he knew was that someone nearby needed help. They sounded like they were a child too, and maybe that's why Timmy ran to try to help them. Or maybe it was because Timmy was starting to not be as afraid as he was before, now that he had traveled through sewers and snuck into a library after-hours and managed to get away from the man in the junkyard and helped to fight off the Dark.

But because Timmy wasn't thinking, we'll never know for sure why he ran towards the sound of the girl shouting for help. What we do know is what he did when he got there.

He stopped so suddenly that his shoes skidded on the street. Down a dead-end alleyway there was a girl around Timmy's age. She had strawberry-blonde hair and her clothes were kind of dirty and her eyes were very wide and afraid.

The alley was already dark, but on each side of the girl were two shapes that were even darker, so inky black that they looked as if you were staring into a bottomless hole. The Dark.

*"Is this the boy we're supposed to fetch?"* said one of the shadows.

*"I'm not sure,"* said the other. *"Whatever it is, it is small and afraid. Total Dark said the boy would be small and afraid. Let's just take this one back with us and see if it's right."*

"I'm not a boy!" the girl cried out. "Someone,

help me!"

Timmy wasn't sure what to do. He didn't have a flasher because he had given his to Mother after her weapon exploded. So instead, he picked up a rock and he threw it at one of the shadows. It passed right through it without doing any harm, but it did get the Dark's attention.

The shadow spun around. *"Hey! Who's throwing stuff? That's not very nice."*

"Get away from her!" Timmy shouted.

The Dark laughed, a horrible grating sound. *"Who's going to make us?"* one of the shadows asked. "You? You're tiny."

*"And scrawny!"* said the other shadow.

"Not me," Timmy said. "My friends."

Bear Company rounded the corner, their flashers raised and set to "burst." Tiny balls of blue light blasted from the ends. The two minions didn't even see it coming; the balls of light shot holes in the shadows until there was nothing left of them.

"Timmy, are you okay?" Mother asked frantically.

"Yes, I'm fine," he said.

"Good. Don't ever run off like that! Do you understand me, young man?" Mother scolded. Timmy stared at the ground. For a small stuffed bear, Mother could be very stern. "Yes, ma'am," he said quietly.

"Excuse me," said the girl at the end of the alley. Her eyes were still very wide—not in fear, but in amazement. "Just what exactly is going on here?"

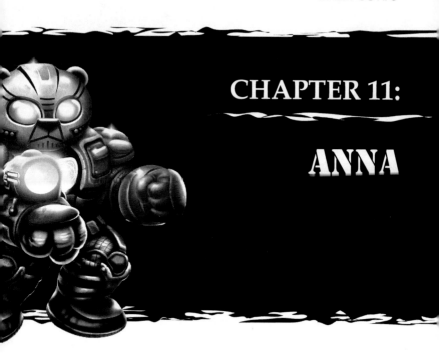

# CHAPTER 11:

# ANNA

The girl in the alley bit hungrily into the apple that Timmy had stowed in his backpack, the one that Sneak took from the man in the junkyard earlier.

"Thank you," she said with her mouth full. "I was starving!"

"Um… I'm sorry for asking," Timmy said,

"but don't you think any of this is strange?"

The girl looked from him to Mother to the other four armored bears standing before her. "What's strange?" she asked.

"You know," he said. "The talking bears with armor and cannons that shoot light?"

"Oh, *that*." The girl shrugged. "Well, I was almost just kidnapped by two talking shadows that thought I was a boy, so my day has been pretty strange already." She took another big bite of apple and said, "I'm Anna, by the way."

"I'm Timmy. And this is Mother, Bruiser, Sneak, Patch, and Blue." He pointed at each of the bears as he named them. Mother nodded. Bruiser folded his arms. Sneak waved hello. Patch smiled (although Anna couldn't see it behind the bear's helmet) and Blue looked away shyly.

"Nice to meet you all," said Anna. "I'm sure glad you came when you did, or else those shadow-things would have taken me away."

"Anna," Mother asked, "what are you doing out here alone at night?"

Anna stared at the brick wall to her left, not wanting to look Mother in the eye. "I sort of… ran away from home."

"I see," said Mother. "Well, we're kind of in a hurry, but there's no way that I can let a young girl walk home alone, especially with the Dark out there. We'll help get you home safely."

Anna shook her head. "I'm sorry, but I'm not going back."

"But your parents are probably worried sick about you!" said Sneak.

"My parents are gone," Anna said sadly. "They passed away when I was little. I'm an orphan. I was in a foster home, but the people there didn't treat me very nicely, so I ran away."

"I'm sorry to hear that about your parents," Mother said quietly.

Timmy didn't say anything, but he was sorry too. He kind of knew how she felt; his own mother had passed away when he was six years old, leaving just him and his father. And as great as Timmy's dad was, he was often away for work, so usually Timmy was alone—at least, until Bear Company came along.

"I was only out here on my own for a few hours when those shadow things tried to nab me," Anna continued. "They kept talking about a boy…" She looked at Timmy and squinted her eyes. "Were they talking about you?"

"It's kind of a long story," Timmy said. It wasn't actually a very long story at all; the truth was that Timmy didn't know exactly why the Dark was after him, but he knew that it had something to do with his dad's experiment and a portal to another world. But he didn't want to say all that to Anna. Instead he said, "I don't understand, though. Why would they attack you?"

"Fear," Mother said simply. "The Dark can smell fear. It's probably how they found us before. And Anna is out here in the city alone, at night; they could smell her fear, too."

"I'm not afraid!" Anna said loudly. From somewhere nearby, a car backfired, and the boom of it made Anna jump. "Okay, fine. I'm a little bit afraid. But only a little."

"That settles it," Mother said. "You're coming with us, Anna. At least until we meet up with Wolf Squad and decide what to do."

"Okay," Anna said. "Where are we going, Mama Bear?"

*"Nowhere,"* said a hissing voice behind

them. Bear Company spun around; at the other end of the alley were several shadows, so dark Timmy couldn't see the street behind them, and they were blocking the only way out.

"Open fire!" Bruiser shouted. He raised his flasher and shot a series of blue balls of light at the shadows, but the Dark wasn't going to fall for that again. They parted quickly and swooped down the alley, across the walls and along the ground. They were very fast, and reminded Timmy of watching sharks swim in the water toward a school of little fish.

Except here in the alley, he and Bear Company were the little fish.

"Form up around Timmy!" Mother said. Even though she had no armor, she still raised her flasher and fired at the coming shadows. Bear Company formed a circle with Timmy and Anna in the center, their five flashers aimed outward.

"They're too fast! I can't hit anything!" Sneak said. Every little blue ball of light he shot missed as the Dark swept around them.

"Set your flashers to cone!" Mother instructed. Each flasher had three settings— the burst, which shot the little balls of light; the beam, which was very strong but needed to charge up for several seconds first; and the cone, which was a very wide, very quick flash of light. The bears had used it once before to defeat several of the Dark at once by all firing the cone at the same time, which had made a huge circle of light with Bear Company at the center.

Unfortunately for them, it didn't work a second time.

Before the bears could even set their flashers, one of the Dark bonded with an aluminum garbage can, wrapping its shadow all the way around it, and then rolled toward them like a bowling ball. The impact sent Bruiser and Blue flying.

Mother turned her flasher dial to "beam" and it made a high-pitched sound as it charged up. *Whhhhiiirrr…* And then she fired: *Shooom!* The beam of light cut the garbage-can shadow in half.

*"Get the boy!"* hissed one of the shadows. Timmy couldn't tell which one spoke, because none of the Dark had mouths. He couldn't even tell how many there were, as they swirled around the bears like a storm, but there had to be at least ten of them. They were outnumbered. They were down a flasher, since Mother's had exploded. And Mother didn't even have her armor.

"We should retreat!" Sneak said. "We can't win this battle!"

"Hyah!" Bruiser tried to punch and kick at the shadows, but his little hands just went straight through them. "Yah! Yah!" Two of the Dark wrapped their shadowy tendrils around his arms, lifted him straight into the air, and flung him across the alley. All Timmy saw was a spinning flash of green as Bruiser sailed overhead, landing with a stupendous crash in a heap of cardboard boxes.

"For once," he said, sounding dizzy, "I agree with Sneak. We should get out of here!"

"Where are we going to retreat to?" Patch asked, shooting a hole in the closest shadow. "There's nowhere for us to run!"

Timmy felt a hand grab onto his arm; it was Anna, clutching him tightly as she tried to look in every direction, her eyes once again wide and fearful.

"It'll be okay," he told her. "Bear Company will get us out." Sometimes people say things that they don't believe themselves, and this was one of those times. Things did not look good for them, and the Dark was daring to get closer.

A black shadowy wisp snaked along the ground and wrapped around Timmy's ankle. Before he could even look down, it yanked him off his feet and began dragging him away.

"Help!" he cried. Without a flasher, there was nothing he could do.

"Timmy!" Mother shouted. She ran towards him with her flasher raised, but without her armor, she wasn't as fast, and she wasn't protected. One of the Dark grabbed onto her feet and flung her back, away from Timmy. Her stuffed, plushy body hit the brick wall at the end of the alley and she fell face-down to the ground. "Timmy…" She held up one paw as he was dragged away toward the mouth of the alley. "What are we going to do now?"

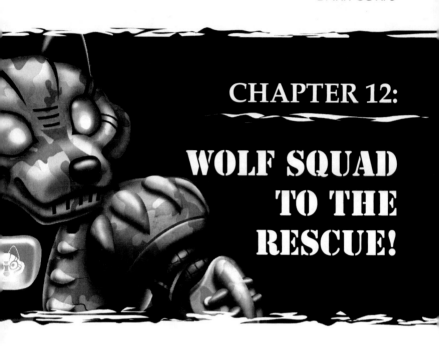

# CHAPTER 12:

# WOLF SQUAD TO THE RESCUE!

"**W**HOOOO-HOOO!"

Timmy heard a loud, jubilant holler, and he saw a flash of gray and a little bit of glowing purple. Then he heard a flasher beam fire—*Shoom!*—and the Dark that was holding onto him suddenly had a very large hole in the center of it. The shadow shrieked and let go of Timmy, slithering quickly up a wall and away.

Timmy, who was still lying on his back on the ground, looked up. Standing before him was a wolf—but nothing like an ordinary wolf. This wolf was about two feet tall, standing upright on two legs, and wearing gray armor. It had a blue flasher on one wrist, and its eyes glowed purple.

"Hiya, Timmy!" the wolf said excitedly. Even though it was wearing a helmet, its mouth was pulled back at the sides in a way that made it look like it was smiling. "It's super great to see you again!"

"Again?" Timmy repeated, confused.

"Listen, you wait right here," the wolf said. "I've gotta go help out. Whooo-hoo!" The wolf hollered again and jumped clear over Timmy as he rejoined the fight. And he wasn't the only one; three more wolves had also appeared to help out.

"That must be Wolf Squad!" Timmy said to himself.

Anna hurried over and helped him to his feet. "Timmy," she said, "you also see four armored wolves that are standing on two legs, right?"

"I do," he said.

"Oh, good." She sighed with relief. "I just wanted to make sure I wasn't the only one."

Now there were nine flashers against the Dark instead of five. In only a few short moments the combination of Bear Company and Wolf Squad had the Dark on the ropes—which is just a fancy way of saying that the Dark was about to be defeated.

*"Retreat!"* hissed one of the shadows.

*"What does 'retreat' mean?"* said another.

*"Run away!"* The Dark slithered across the walls and vanished, one by one, into an open sewer grate.

A wolf with blue eyes started toward the sewer grate. "We should go after them and finish them off!" he growled.

Another wolf, this one with green eyes, put a hand on the other wolf's shoulder. "No, Clunker. Let them run. They'll think twice before they attack again." The wolf with green eyes turned to Timmy. "I must say, it is very good to see you again, Timmy."

"I'm sorry," Timmy replied, "but I don't think we've met before."

The wolf chuckled. "Oh, we have. Just not like this." His armor retracted with a sound like *shooop*, and Timmy's mouth fell open a little. Standing before him was a plushy stuffed wolf.

"I *do* remember you," Timmy said. The last time they moved, before coming to the city, Timmy's dad had given him a gift of four stuffed wolves. At the time, Timmy didn't understand why he needed four wolves instead of just one, but now he did; they were the members of Wolf

Squad, and just like Bear Company, Timmy's dad had built them to help protect him and fight against the Dark.

The wolf put his armor back on—*zip-zip!*—and then laughed again. "Yes, last time you saw us we looked a lot different. We couldn't even talk! But now I can tell you: my name is Chomper, and I'm the leader of Wolf Squad."

"Nice to meet you, Chomper," said Timmy. He looked from one wolf to the next. All four of them looked almost identical—they were all the same height, and they all wore gray and black armor with a camouflage pattern on it, just like soldiers do. The only way to tell them apart was their different colored eyes; Chomper's were green, and then there were red, blue, and the purple one that had saved him from the Dark. Each of them had a flasher on their wrist and a symbol on their chest that glowed the same color as their eyes.

Chomper pointed to the wolf with red eyes and said, "That's Zipper. He's a climbing expert. If you need to get up high, he's your guy." He then pointed to the wolf with blue eyes and said, "That's Clunker, and he can fix anything mechanical. He could build a helicopter out of a dining room set and an outboard motor." Finally, there was the purple one. "And that's Nutter."

"What does he do?" Timmy asked.

"Um… well, Nutter is a just a little nutty," Chomper admitted. "But we like to have him around because he's good in a fight, and he makes us laugh."

Nutter shrugged. "I'm also very good at standing on my head."

Chomper looked over at Anna. "And who is this lovely young lady?"

Anna's cheeks turned pink. "I'm Anna. The

bears saved me from the shadows, but then we were attacked again."

"Anna? Well, I believe we met your friend Jonathan," said Chomper.

Anna gasped. "You saw Jonathan? Is he okay?"

"He's okay," said the blue-eyed wolf. "He'll be very glad to know that you're safe." "How did you find us?" Mother asked as she brushed dirt and dust from her furry belly.

Chomper explained, "The general told us that you were stranded in the junkyard, so we went there first. Of course, you had already left by then. So Clunker fixed up an old car for us—"

"You *drove* here?" Mother said, shocked. "Are you crazy?"

"No," said Chomper. "Nutter is the crazy one."

"What if someone saw you?" Mother

demanded.

"Nobody saw us," Chomper said. "Don't worry. The windows were tinted dark."

"Yeah," Clunker chimed in. "I worked the pedals while Nutter steered."

"But then I crashed into a pole," said Nutter.

"And then we saw all these flashing blue lights," added Zipper, "and that's how we found you."

"I see," said Mother. "Well, we did just put on quite a light show. If you saw it, then chances are good that some people did, too. They may be on their way here right now. We should get moving."

"I agree," said Chomper. "But we can't take the car because we crashed, and we can't go underground because that's where the Dark went…"

"And we can't just walk out on the street,"

said Mother. "So do you have any ideas?"

"I have an idea," said Zipper. "We go up."

"Up?" said both Timmy and Mother at the same time.

"That's right," said Zipper. "Up."

# CHAPTER 13:

# UP

The eleven of them—the five bears of Bear Company, the four wolves of Wolf Squad, and Timmy and Anna—climbed up the fire escape of the building in the alley, being careful to be as silent as possible because the stairs were metal and the wolves' and bears' armor clanked a little bit with each step.

Wolf Squad went up first, followed by Anna,

and then Timmy, and then Bear Company. The building was very tall, and they had to move slowly, so it felt like it took a very long time to reach the top—but eventually they got to the wide, flat roof. Unfortunately, Timmy couldn't see anywhere else for them to go. They certainly couldn't jump from rooftop to rooftop.

"Great," said Bruiser to Zipper. "Now what, genius?"

"I'll show you," Zipper replied. He stepped right up to the edge of the roof and held out his left arm. There was an odd sound—*thwip!*—and a thin cord shot from Zipper's wrist, across the empty space between the buildings, and stuck with a *smack* on the opposite rooftop.

"Hey Timmy," said Zipper, "have you ever been zip-lining?"

"Yes, I have," Timmy answered. Once, when they had lived in the countryside, his dad had taken him zip-lining—which was basically a strong cable that was connected to something on both sides. Timmy had to wear a helmet and a safety harness, and then he zipped across the cable between two tall trees. It was a lot of fun, and it was very, very different from zipping between two buildings, more than a hundred feet up in the air with no net underneath him.

"That's what we'll be doing here," said Zipper. "We can just zip from rooftop to rooftop."

"Oh, fun!" Anna said. She bounced excitedly on her heels. "Can I go first?"

"I don't think so, little lady," said Chomper. "We have to make sure this line is safe first. I'll go first."

"No way," Bruiser said, pushing his way to the front. "I'll go first. Besides, I'm the bravest one here."

Chomper laughed a little. "Sure thing,

Bruiser. Go right ahead."

Zipper gave the green bear a harness. Bruiser slipped his legs through it, tightened it securely around him, and then attached it to the cable. "Okay," he said. "Here I go." Then he looked down, and Timmy was pretty sure he heard Bruiser gulp—which was very strange indeed, because he was also pretty sure that Bruiser didn't have a real throat to gulp with.

"We don't have all night," Zipper said.

"I'm going!" Bruiser snapped. "And by the way, we didn't need your help. We had it handled!" Then he jumped. The tiny pulley at the top of the harness made a *zzziiiiipp* sound as the small green bear soared quickly between the buildings, his short legs kicking in the air. "Aaaaaaahhh!" Bruiser cried out. Then he reached the opposite rooftop and collapsed in a heap.

"Bruiser!" Mother called out. "Are you okay?"

"Nothing to it!" Bruiser shouted back. "Easy as pie!"

"Okay, Anna. Now you can go," said Chomper. He helped her into a harness and attached it to the line. She took a deep breath, held it, and pushed off the rooftop.

"Wheee!" she called out as she zipped across to the next building. Once her feet were on solid ground, she cheered and shouted, "That was so much fun!"

Next Chomper sent Patch and Sneak, and then Clunker and Nutter. When it was Nutter's turn, he didn't put on a harness; he simply grabbed onto the cable with his hands and zipped across, shouting a "whooo-hoo!" as he went.

Mother pointed her paw at Timmy and said, "Don't you even *think* about doing that, mister."

Timmy shook his head. "Of course not!"

"Okay, Timmy, it's your turn," said Chomper. "Then I'll send Mother, then me, and Zipper will go last."

Chomper helped Timmy into the harness and tightened it around his legs and waist. "Can the Dark get to us up here?" Timmy asked him.

Chomper shook his head. "I don't think so," he said. "But I don't know for sure. There's a lot we don't know about them yet. For now, let's just worry about getting you across safely."

Once the harness was on, Timmy stood at the edge of the rooftop and looked down. He wasn't afraid of heights, but this was very different; there was nothing below him, nothing to catch him. Far, far down he could see cars driving by on the street and, if he squinted, he could even see people walking.

"Come on, Timmy!" Anna yelled. "It's

okay! There's nothing to be afraid of!"

"Right," Timmy said to himself. "There's nothing to be afraid of. Nothing to be afraid of at all… except that I'm very high up and there's nothing under me."

Then he felt a warm paw on his arm. "Are you okay?" Mother asked.

"Can… can you push me?" he asked her.

She looked very surprised. "What?"

"Push me? Please?" he asked nicely.

"Timmy… Are you asking me to push you off a building?"

He nodded. "Yes."

"Well, okay. If you want me to," Mother said. "Don't look down; look over at Anna. Just look at her."

"Okay," Timmy said. He looked over at Anna on the opposite rooftop. She was smiling and waving her hand for him to come over to them. Then he felt two strong paws on his back. The next thing he knew, the wind was rushing in his ears. He was off the rooftop, out over nothing, zipping along towards Anna, who was getting bigger and bigger by the moment as he got closer and closer. Then, in just a few seconds, he was there. She and Sneak helped him down and unclipped his harness.

"See?" said Anna. "Nothing to it, right?"

"Yeah," Timmy agreed. He was smiling so wide that his mouth hurt a little. "Nothing to it."

Two minutes later, their entire group was on the next rooftop. Zipper went last, and after he joined them he disconnected his cord and wound it up back into his wrist armor, like reeling in a fishing line.

Blue checked the map of the city in his helmet and said, "Okay, just nine more rooftops and then we can climb back down. Then we'll be out of the city."

"We have to do that nine more times?" Timmy asked.

"No," said Anna. "We *get* to do that nine more times. How exciting! I sure am glad you found me in that alley."

"And I'm sure glad that Wolf Squad found us in that alley," Mother said. "I don't even want to think of what could have happened if they didn't."

"We didn't need them to come save us," said Bruiser angrily. "We had it under control!"

"Same old Bruiser." Chomper shook his head and said to Timmy, "He wants to be the fiercest fighter in the Dark Corps, but you know what he really is? The biggest attitude in the Dark Corps."

"What?!" Bruiser growled and balled his small fists. "I'll show you an attitude…"

"Boys!" Mother said sharply. "Play nice!"

"Yes, Mother," said both Chomper and Bruiser at the same time.

"I'm sorry," said Timmy, "but what is the Dark Corps?"

"Oh, that's what the general calls us," Chomper told him. "Not just Bear Company and Wolf Squad, but Corps Command and all the others too—together we're the Dark Corps, because we fight off the Dark."

"I see," said Timmy. "How many of you are there?"

"Oh, there are lots," said Zipper, "and they're stationed all over the place to help you get to where you have to go. You'll probably meet them all."

"I hope I do," said Timmy. Over the last four years, ever since his mother passed away and he and his father started moving around so much,

Timmy had gotten a lot of stuffed animals as gifts from his dad. Some were jungle animals, others were desert animals, and still others were farm animals. Timmy wondered if every one of them were members of the Dark Corps. And if they were, he couldn't wait to see them again.

"I think that's enough chatter," said Chomper. "Come on, we have a lot more zip-lining to do!"

# CHAPTER 14:

# CALIBRATE THE RHODODENDRONS

**I**n the wide, white underground lab, Dr. Barnes was hard at work trying to fashion a proper boat out of his wooden desk. The two shadows, Blot and Pitch, watched his every move, and they asked a lot of questions. However, Dr. Barnes had found that if he used very big words and made them sound like very smart answers, the Dark would pretend that what he was doing made perfect sense, because nobody likes to look dumb, not even shadowy creatures from another dimension.

For example, when he was making oars out of the legs of his desk, Blot hissed, *"Why are you doing that?"*

And Dr. Barnes answered, "Well, I need these capacitors in order to properly calibrate the rhododendrons, or else the escape velocity will be terminally unpalatable." Most of those words are pretty large, but if you knew even what one or two of them meant, you would know that what Dr. Barnes said was complete and utter nonsense.

But Blot did not know what any of those words meant, so he simply said, *"I see. Of course. That makes perfect sense. Keep working!"*

While Dr. Barnes worked on making the boat, Arjun continued to work on building their portal, and he too decided to get in on the fun. When Pitch asked him what a screwdriver was, Arjun said, "Ah, well, this is called a microwave, and you use it to pontificate on the omnibuses until they are dehydrated."

*"Right,"* said Pitch. *"I knew that. I just wanted to see if YOU knew that."*

Dr. Barnes had to try very hard not to laugh, because it would ruin their entire plan if the Dark knew that he and Arjun were making fun of them. And in order to keep himself from laughing, Dr. Barnes thought of his young son Timmy. He knew that Bear Company was with him, because one of Total Dark's minions had reported back about the five small armored bears that fought them off with weapons that shot pure light. Dr. Barnes very much wished that he could get a message to Timmy, or Bear Company, or even the general. He hoped that the bears were at least out of the city; in fact, they should have made it to the farmhouse by now, unless something terrible had happened.

"Don't worry, Timmy. I'm coming for you," Dr. Barnes said to himself.

*"What did you say?"* Blot asked.

"Oh, I said, 'Blot, can you please hand me that watermelon?' No, not that one; that's a cannoli. Yes, that one. That's the watermelon. Thank you."

Arjun almost snorted as Blot handed the doctor a tape measure.

\* \* \*

Ms. Gertrude was still not very happy, and now she was also very frustrated.

She stood at the mouth of a dead-end alley. It was an appropriate place for her to be standing, because her search for Timothy Barnes had also reached a dead end. She had gone to the junkyard, but that wasn't much help. The man that owned it just kept talking about armored bears that walked and talked and tied him up with a rubber hose. But the man had described the boy, and it sounded like it could have been Timmy.

Ms. Gertrude looked around the entire junkyard, but she didn't find anything—or rather, she *almost* didn't find anything. She did find a small hole cut in a section of the fence at the very back of the junkyard, and the hole was just wide enough for a small boy to crawl through.

On the other side of the junkyard there was a park, which might seem like a good place for a boy to be, but she searched the entire park and found nothing. Then she heard some people talking about flashing blue lights in an alleyway downtown. By then it was dark, and the people said that the blue lights looked like a small lightning storm. Ms. Gertrude went to the alley, but there was nothing there.

She walked all the way down to the end of the alleyway, but there was nothing to see except for a couple of knocked-over trash cans.

"Oh, hello there," she said as she spotted something on the ground at the far end. She bent over and picked up a small clump of red fuzz. She had no doubt that this little bit of fur had come off of one of Timmy's toy bears.

She wasn't far from the edge of the city, which could only mean that Timothy Barnes was close to escaping. And once he was out of the city, he would be much, much harder for her to find.

It was late, and Ms. Gertrude was tired, and hungry, and not at all happy, but she was also determined. "I'm going to find you, Timothy," she said out loud. "And then we'll see all about these talking bears."

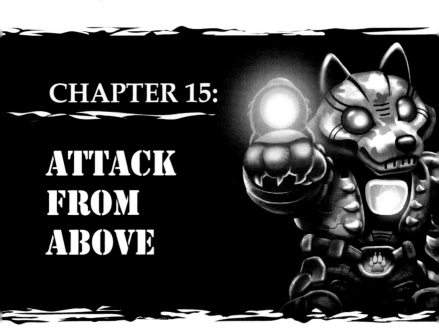

# CHAPTER 15:

# ATTACK FROM ABOVE

**B**y the time Timmy had zip-lined across to the fourth building, he was no longer afraid. Mother didn't have to push him off the edge anymore. By the time he zip-lined across to the sixth building, he was actually having fun. And by the time they zip-lined to the ninth and final building, Timmy was a little sad, because he wanted to keep doing it. All this zip-lining made him forget all about being chased by the Dark, and what might have happened to his dad, and what could still happen if they didn't get out of the city soon.

But as his father had once told him, "All good things must come to an end," which is a fancy way of saying that if everything was good all the time, we would have no way to truly appreciate how good a thing really was when a good thing came along.

"Look!" said Patch, pointing over the edge of the rooftop. "It's the end of the city." She was right; they were on top of the last of the tall buildings of the city. Across the street was where the suburbs began, which was an area where all the houses were normal-sized with backyards and swing-sets and driveways. Because it was nighttime, Timmy couldn't see past the suburbs, but he knew that beyond that, far in the distance, were wide, green farm fields and gently rolling hills.

"What are we waiting for?" Timmy said excitedly. "Let's go!"

"Whoa, hold up there, buckaroo," said Chomper. "Maybe it would be best if we waited until morning. I don't think the Dark can get to us up here."

"He's right," said Mother. "It's risky to have people see us, but it's even riskier to be on the ground where the Dark can attack. They must know that we're trying to leave the city."

"And there are still too many shadowy places for them to hide," Blue added. "Out in the country, there will be far fewer places that the Dark can get to us."

"I guess you're right," said Timmy. "Hey, maybe Patch can finish fixing you before morning comes."

"I sure can!" said Patch. "It'll just take a little bit of time."

"Clunker can help," said Chomper. "He's great at fixing things."

Timmy's stomach rumbled. "I'm getting hungry again," he said.

"Me too," Anna agreed. "I hope in the morning we can find some breakfast."

"Wait," said Zipper. "Does anyone else hear that?"

All four of the wolves of Wolf Squad listened intently, their mechanical ears twitching left and right. Wolves—real, normal wolves in the wild and in zoos—have excellent hearing, and Wolf Squad had even better hearing than that, on account of their high-tech armor.

"What is that?" Chomper asked quietly.

Soon the bears could hear it too, as each

member of Bear Company began looking left and right, and even up above them, trying to find the source of the sound.

"It sounds like… birds," said Patch.

"Whatever it is, it's getting closer," said Sneak.

"I don't hear anything," Timmy told them.

"Me neither," Anna agreed.

But soon even they could hear it. Patch was right; it did sound like birds, several of them, all beating their wings—but it was much louder than a bird's wings, and usually when something is louder, it means it's also bigger.

"Look!" Timmy pointed at the sky. There, against the bluish-black and the stars and the dim moonlight, they could see several shadows of inky black, much darker than the night sky behind them.

It was the Dark.

There were at least a dozen of them, roughly the shape of bats but larger than any bird Timmy had ever seen. They flapped their large black wings as they came closer and closer to the rooftop.

"Aw, come on!" Bruiser complained. "Some of the Dark can *fly?* That's not fair at all!"

One of the shadows must have spotted them, because it let out a loud, horrible shriek: *"Skreeeee!"*

The other flying Dark joined in the call and in seconds the sky was filled with the piercing screech. The flying Dark circled the rooftop, keeping their distance, flying so quickly, around and around and around, that they looked like a dark black maelstrom—which is a fancy word for a whirlpool or cyclone or any other force of nature that whips around in a frenzied circle.

"We're cornered," said Chomper glumly.

"We have nowhere to go, and we'd never climb down fast enough!"

"Then the only thing we can do is fight!" Bruiser shouted. He raised up his flasher and fired a burst of light, *thoom-thoom-thoom-thoom,* but the flying Dark simply veered left or right, avoiding the blue balls of light.

"Everyone, fire!" Mother commanded. All nine flashers raised skyward and fired. Light danced across the sky as the tiny balls of light flew past the flying Dark, missing them. They were too fast.

Then, one by one, the Dark folded back their inky black wings and nosedived down toward the rooftop.

"Wolf Squad, concentrate on the divers!" Chomper instructed. The four wolves all fired at the closest Dark as it banked down toward them. It tried to veer left, but Nutter was already shooting in that direction; his flasher pierced the shadow. The flying Dark screeched in pain, its shadow riddled with small holes. It tumbled down to the rooftop and crashed.

Clunker charged up his beam… *Whhhhiiirrr*… Then he fired: *Shooom!* The shadow was gone.

"Ha, we got one!" Nutter laughed and danced a little.

"Hey, pay attention!" Chomper snapped. "There are plenty more where that came—"

"Help!" Anna cried. One of the flying Dark swooped down and reached out with tendrils of shadow. She tried to run, but there was nowhere else for her to go. The Dark wrapped its inky wisps around her shoulders and lifted her off the rooftop. "Mama Bear, help me!" she called out.

"Anna!" Mother raised her flasher to shoot down the Dark, but she stopped; if she hit it,

Anna would fall.

*"Is this the right one?"* the flying Dark asked its cohorts.

*"I don't think it is,"* said another shadow. *"The one we're after has dark hair. This one has an ugly light color."*

"My hair is not ugly!" Anna insisted as she struggled to get free from the Dark. "Let me go!"

*"Do what it says,"* said a shadow. *"Let it go."*

"Wait, don't—" Anna tried to say, but it was too late. The flying Dark released her, and she began to fall. Her breath caught in her throat; she couldn't even scream for help.

"I got her!" Zipper ran to the edge of the rooftop and, without thinking, jumped off. He caught Anna as she fell, and then he fired his grappling hook from his wrist back toward the rooftop. But the hook missed; it soared through the air but didn't stick to anything.

"Nutter, grab it!" Mother shouted.

The purple-eyed wolf jumped and grabbed the grappling hook while it was still in the air. Clunker, seeing that his friend was also going to fall, grabbed onto Nutter, and Chomper grabbed onto him. Then Sneak grabbed onto Chomper, and Patch grabbed onto Sneak. Blue grabbed Sneak by his orange legs, and finally Bruiser, annoyed that he had to save *everyone,* grabbed onto Blue and pulled with all his might.

All of Wolf Squad was hanging off the side of the building, with Zipper and Anna at the far end of his rope, and most of Bear Company held on at the rooftop to make sure they didn't fall.

"Everyone, pull!" said Mother. "Pull as hard as you can!" Slowly but surely, the bears started to pull up Chomper, and Nutter, and finally Zipper and Anna.

But while all this was happening, no one was paying any attention to the Dark, because they were more concerned for their friends' safety. And since no one was watching, they didn't see two of the flying Dark swoop down and each grab Timmy by an arm—until he was already a few feet in the air.

"Mother!" Timmy shouted.

Mother gasped. She ran as fast as her soft, plushy legs could carry her and jumped. She just barely managed to grab onto one of Timmy's sneakers with her left paw, and she dangled there as the Dark flew up, higher and higher into the night sky.

*"Is this the right child?"* one of the shadows hissed.

*"Hmm… small, scared, dark hair… yes, I believe this is the one,"* said the other shadow that had hold of Timmy's arm.

*"And what is that thing attached to it?"* the first shadow asked, referring to Mother.

*"I'm not sure. It sure is ugly, though."*

"Hey!" Mother shouted. "That's not nice!" She raised her right arm and fired her flasher upward, hitting one of the shadows and making a neat little hole in it.

*"OW! That hurt!"* the shadow screeched.

"Mother, be careful!" Timmy said. "If they drop us…"

She looked down. They were indeed very high in the air; Wolf Squad and the rest of Bear Company looked like teeny-tiny toys from up here.

Down on the rooftop, Chomper watched the Dark fly away with Timmy and Mother. "It's over, then," he said sadly. "We failed. There's no way we can get to them now."

"Don't say that just yet," said Blue. He had

not told anyone, but while they were zip-lining, he was able to get a radio signal to the general, and he knew that they had even more help than just Wolf Squad.

High in the air, Mother held on to Timmy's sneaker by just one paw. If she could hold on until they got to wherever it was they were going, maybe she could still protect him. Maybe…

Suddenly there was another sound in the air, a sound that was not the beating of giant bat-like wings. It sounded sort of like a jet engine, except that jet engines are very, very loud, and this one was not so loud; and usually when something doesn't sound as loud as it should, it means it's smaller.

Mother smiled. "Well, how about that. It looks like Blue called in an Air Strike."

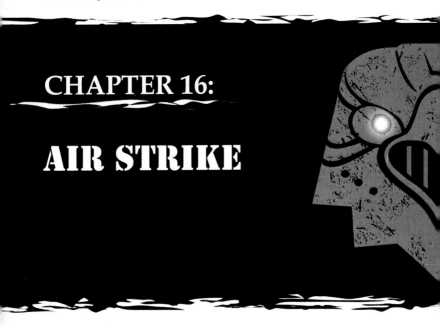

# CHAPTER 16:

# AIR STRIKE

**A**ll Timmy saw was a blur of red shooting past them so quickly he couldn't even tell what it was. Then there was an orange blur, and finally a green blur.

"What are they?" Timmy asked.

"They," Mother said happily, "are the birds of Air Strike."

The red blur circled back around and leveled out its large wings. It was an eagle—but not an actual eagle. It was an armored eagle, its red feathers and glowing red eyes shining in the moonlight. On each of its wings was a flasher.

To the eagle's left was an orange falcon, and to its right was a green hawk, both of which also had flashers attached to their wings. They flew in a V formation toward the flying Dark, and when they were close enough they fired their flashers and destroyed the Dark in no time.

Of course, that was very bad news for Timmy and Mother, because they suddenly found themselves falling through the air. But the birds of Air Strike folded back their wings and shot like bullets after them. The eagle caught Timmy in his red talons, and the falcon caught Mother's arms.

A few seconds later, they landed safely back on the rooftop. Anna ran over to Timmy and threw her arms around his neck, squeezing him in a tight hug.

"I'm so glad you're safe!" she said. "And you too, Mama Bear." She looked over at the three majestic armored birds and said, "More friends of yours, Timmy?"

"Yeah," he said. "More friends." To the red eagle, Timmy said, "Thank you for saving me. I don't know what we would've done without you."

"You're welcome," said the eagle. "But we cannot stay; we need to go after the rest of the flying Dark and make sure they don't return to their base and report what happened here. The less they know about the Dark Corps, the easier your journey will be. Goodbye for now, Timmy. Just know that we will always be close by if you need us."

The three birds opened their great, metallic wings and took off into the air with a sound like a small jet engine. In seconds they were gone.

"Who was that?" Timmy asked as he watched them fly away.

"That was Eagle-Eye and his Air Strike team," Mother told him. "They patrol the skies and report to Corps Command. I have a feeling we'll see them again soon."

"I hope we do," Timmy said.

"Well," said Chomper, "I don't know about the rest of you, but I think we should get off this rooftop. I'm feeling a bit exposed."

The eleven of them climbed down the fire escape on the side of the building. Once they were on solid ground again, Bruiser got down on his hands and knees and kissed the sidewalk.

"I'm so happy not to be so high up!" he said.

"Bruiser, are you afraid of heights?" Timmy asked.

"I'm not afraid of anything!" he said. "But... heights do make me a little nervous. Just a little."

There was almost nobody out on the streets this time of night, but still the group of them hid behind a building, between two dumpsters, while Patch and Clunker finally finished fixing up Mother. When they were done, she stood up straight and tried out her armor. The case on her back opened up and the pieces slid over her plushy body, all shiny and bright.

"Ah! That's much better," said Mother. "Thank you, Patch. Thank you, Clunker."

"Aw, shucks. It was nothing," said Clunker.

"Alright," said Chomper. "There's only about an hour or so before the sun rises. If you hurry, you can get through the suburbs and into the countryside before people start waking up."

Timmy couldn't believe his ears. "Aren't you coming with us?" he asked Chomper.

The leader of Wolf Squad shook his head. "I'm afraid not, Timmy. You remember that some of the Dark ran away into the sewers, right? Well, they're going to keep looking for you, and they might try to take other children like they tried to take Jonathan and Anna. It's our duty to make sure they're protected too. We're going to stay here in the city and see to it that the Dark doesn't take anyone."

Timmy nodded. Even though he wanted very much for Wolf Squad to come with them, he knew it was important that no other child was taken by the Dark.

"Don't worry," said Chomper. "You're in very good hands with Bear Company." Then he turned to Anna and said, "You can stay here in the city with us, if you want. We'll make sure you're safe."

"Thank you," Anna said, "but there's nothing here for me. Besides, I've had a greater adventure in just the last few hours than I have in my whole life! I think I'm going to stay with Bear Company and Timmy and see where this story goes." Then her cheeks turned pink and she added, "If that's okay with you, Mama Bear."

Mother nodded. "Of course it's okay."

"Alright then," said Chomper. "This is where we say goodbye."

Timmy and Anna both gave each member of Wolf Squad a hug—including Nutter, who squirmed a little bit—and then Bear Company said goodbye to their friends, too. Even Bruiser shook hands with Chomper and mumbled, "I guess it was kind of nice having you guys around."

Then Wolf Squad went one way, and Bear

Company went the other, crossing the street and finally leaving the city. They made their way as quickly and quietly as they could, and as the first rays of dawn tinted the sky orange, they had made it to the first wide, green field of farmland on the other side.

"So," said Mother, "I suppose the first thing we need to do is find some breakfast for you two. And then we'll go to our next rendezvous point."

"Sounds good," said Timmy. He didn't bother asking where the next meeting place was; the bears didn't seem to want to tell him.

"It's an old farmhouse," said Mother. "There we'll meet up with another unit of Dark Corps who can help us."

"A farmhouse?" said Anna. "Sounds nice. I bet the Dark can't get to us there. They won't even be able to find us! Right?"

"Right," said Mother, though she didn't

sound entirely sure. "Anyway, let's find something to eat. I bet there are some fruit trees around here. Maybe we can find some apples or some plums…"

"How about a bacon tree?" Anna asked. "I could really go for some bacon."

Timmy and the bears laughed. The city was behind them, it was daytime, and he was with his friends. And soon he would see his dad again. At least he hoped.

\* \* \*

From the edge of a sewer grate, the shadow called Blackout watched the armored wolves part ways with the five bears and the two children. He hissed softly; there was nothing he wanted more than to attack, to get his revenge… but the sun was up, and the light was dangerous. No matter;

he knew that the Dark was out there, beyond the city, lurking in the shadows and seeking the boy. Even if he could leave the sewer, Blackout was weakened. The wolves had hurt him with their cannons that fired pure light; his inky black body was riddled with small holes.

*"It will be dark again,"* said a shadow behind him. After Blackout fled from the house and the wolves, he had gone to the sewers, where he found the other Dark that had managed to escape the fight. *"Will we follow when it is safe?"*

*"No,"* Blackout hissed. *"We have unfinished business in this city."* He didn't know why, but the wolves were staying here. They didn't follow the bears and the boy. No doubt to hunt him and the other Dark, he thought. This was no longer about the boy; Blackout's mind was bent on revenge against those that had hurt him.

*"But the boy is gone,"* another shadow

protested. *"Our orders from Total Dark are to capture the boy—"* The Dark did not get to finish his statement. Blackout swooped quickly over the smaller shadow and, in seconds, engulfed it, absorbing the lesser Dark. The holes in his body where the light had hurt him began to close.

He turned to the other Dark. They shrank back; they were also wounded from the battle with the bears and in no shape for a fight. *"Would anyone else like to tell me what we are supposed to be doing?"*

None of the Dark spoke.

*"Good,"* he said. He turned back toward the open sewer grate. What a horrible world this was, with its light and sun and brightness. He wondered if Total Dark would figure out a way to destroy that orange ball in the sky.

If not… perhaps it was time for someone new to take over command of the Dark.

Perhaps it was time for Total Dark to be absorbed.

Either way, he decided, the Dark would conquer this world of light.

# END
# OF
# BOOK
# TWO

# BEAR COMPANY
### will return in
### DARK CORPS SERIES
### BOOK 3

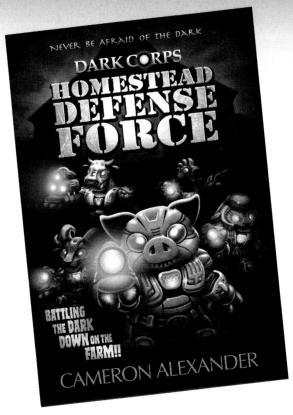

BICKERING
OWLS
PUBLISHING

www.bickeringowls.com

## About the Author

**Cameron Alexander** is the pen name of a mysterious wizard from a different time and a different world. Search for him if you can and if you find him, let me know. He owes me 10 dollars.

Made in United States
Cleveland, OH
10 December 2024

11653083R00092